Lydia

the Reading

Fairy

To book lovers everywhere

Special thanks to Rachel Elliot

ISBN 978-0-545-85207-4

10 9 8 7 6 5 4 3 2 1   16 17 18 19 20

Printed in the U.S.A.   40
First edition, July 2016

Lydia
the Reading
Fairy

by Daisy Meadows

SCHOLASTIC INC.

The Fairyland Palace

Fairyland School

Tippington Town

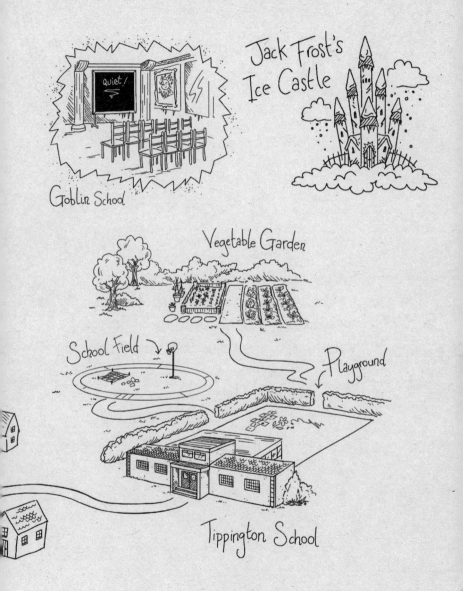

Goblin School

Jack Frost's Ice Castle

Quiet!

Vegetable Garden

School Field

Playground

Tippington School

It's time the School Day Fairies see
How wonderful a school should be—
A place where goblins must be bossed,
And learn about the great Jack Frost.

Now every fairy badge of gold
Makes goblins do as they are told.
Let silly fairies whine and wail.
My cleverness will never fail!

Contents

Backward Books

"I love the smell of libraries, don't you?" said Kirsty Tate.

She took a deep breath and looked around at the bookshelves of the Tippington School library. Her best friend, Rachel Walker, smiled at her.

"I love having you here at school with me," she said. "I wish it was for longer than a week!"

It was only the third day of the new school year, and it had already turned into the most fun and exciting time at school that Rachel had ever known. She had lots of friends at Tippington School, but none of them were as special as Kirsty. She had often wished that they could go to the same school. Then Kirsty's school had been flooded, and the repairs were going to take a week. So for five happy days the best friends were at school together at last.

"It's turning into quite a week, though," Kirsty replied with a grin.

Rachel knew that Kirsty was talking about the extraordinary secret they shared. From the time they had met on Rainspell Island, they had been friends of Fairyland. Even though they had often had magical adventures since then, it was always thrilling to meet brand-new fairy friends. And on the first day of this school year, they had been introduced to the School Day Fairies.

"I wonder if we'll see any of the School Day Fairies today," Kirsty whispered.

Before Rachel could reply, her teacher clapped his hands together to get everyone's attention.

"I want each of you to choose a book to read," said Mr. Beaker. "Then write a few sentences about what you think of the book. All the book reports will be included in the display for the school superintendent's visit."

"What kind of book should we choose?" asked Adam.

"Try to pick something that you think will transport you to another world," said Mr. Beaker. "I love reading, and the best books are the ones where the story comes to life. The people should seem as real to you as your best friend."

The children started to wander around the library, browsing the shelves.

"Be brave in your book choice," Mr. Beaker went on. "It might be exciting to pick something that you wouldn't normally read. Surprise yourself!"

There was a loud crash, and Amina and Ellie jumped back from the shelves they had been browsing. Three heavy books had almost landed on top of them.

"Please be careful," said Mr. Beaker.

"But they just fell off the shelf," cried Ellie. "We didn't touch them!"

"Mr. Beaker, this book is stuck shut," said Adam, who was trying to look at a mystery story. "I can't open it."

Rachel had just chosen a book called *The Princess in the Tower*. But when she opened it, none of the sentences made sense. She blinked a few times, wondering if her eyes were playing tricks on her. But there was definitely something very strange about the book.

"Everything is backward," she whispered to Kirsty. "Listen to how the story begins: 'After ever happily lived Rose Princess.' Something bad has

happened in here.
The books are all
wrong—and I bet
I know why."

Kirsty knew
exactly what her
best friend was
thinking. This was
all happening because
of Jack Frost's goblins!

When the girls had met Marissa
the Science Fairy on the first day of
school, she had whisked them away to
Fairyland. There, the other School Day
Fairies had explained that Jack Frost had
stolen their magical gold star badges.
Without them, lessons would be messed
up and boring.

"Jack Frost has caused so much trouble

for the School Day Fairies," Kirsty
said in a low voice. "We've helped
Marissa the Science Fairy and Alison
the Art Fairy get their badges back, but
we have to find all four of them
to make sure everything is perfect for
the royal visit."

Queen Titania and King Oberon
were planning to pay a visit to the fairy
school. The fairies wanted everything
to be perfect for their beloved king and
queen, but without their magical badges,
the royal visit would be a disaster. Not
only that, but school in the human world
would be ruined, too.

Jack Frost had used the magical badges
to open a school for goblins, where he
was teaching them all about himself. He
thought it was the only subject worth

learning! But when he had expelled two of his students for misbehaving, they had stolen the magical badges from him and taken them to the human world.

And right now, those pesky goblins were in Tippington School!

A Shocking School Visitor

The girls had soon realized that the two new boys in their class were not really boys at all. Their disguise had fooled Mr. Beaker and the other children, but Kirsty and Rachel were very good at recognizing goblins.

"We should find the goblins and see what they're doing," Rachel whispered.

Kirsty nodded. Mr. Beaker wasn't watching them—he was too busy trying to open Adam's book. The girls made their way toward the back of the library, where the lights were dim and the least-borrowed books were kept. Not many students looked in this section, but now the girls could hear loud, screeching voices. They looked at each other.

"Goblins," they said together.

They peered around a tall bookshelf and saw the two goblins sitting cross-legged on the

floor. Each of
them was
holding a
book and
reading
aloud.
They
didn't seem
to care that the
other one wasn't listening.

"Once upon a time
there was a grumpy troll
who liked to eat princes and princesses,"
read the first goblin in a loud voice.
"But there weren't enough princes and
princesses to fill him up. So he decided
to go on a trip with his best friend, a
handsome goblin."

"Milly, Tilly, and Jilly were sisters,"

read the second goblin in an equally loud voice. "They were human beings, and so of course they were annoying and ugly. One day a happy little goblin was stealing some apples when the silly sisters decided to try to stop him."

"They just love the sound of their own voices, don't they!" said Rachel.

"Yes," said Kirsty with a frown, "and it sounds as if those stories have been changed—they don't sound right at all."

Just then they heard footsteps behind them, and they whirled around. Mr. Beaker was coming their way. When he saw the girls and heard the voices, he stopped. Rachel and Kirsty thought that he might scold the goblins, but he just smiled.

"I'm glad to hear that someone in the class is enjoying their books," he said. "I don't know what's gone wrong, but reading doesn't seem to be very much fun today."

"Do you want us to ask them to talk more quietly?" Kirsty asked.

Mr. Beaker shook his head.

"It's nice to hear that they're so enthusiastic," he said. "I don't mind the noise."

15

As he walked away, the girls exchanged a surprised glance.

"I guess the main thing is that they're not causing any trouble," said Rachel. "For now!"

"Look at that bookshelf over there," said Kirsty.

She pointed to a bookshelf in the corner. One of the shelves seemed to be gleaming with a faint light, and the girls hurried toward it.

"The light must be coming from one of the books on this shelf," said Rachel.

"It looks just like a fairy glow."

They searched through the books that were on the shelf until they found one that was shimmering with a golden light.

"This must be the one," said Rachel, taking it down from the shelf. She opened it, and out fluttered Lydia the Reading Fairy! Her black hair was tied in a thick side braid, and she was wearing flowery shorts with a pink sweater.

"Hello, Rachel! Hello, Kirsty!" said Lydia. "Queen Titania told me that you were in the library, and I thought it was the perfect moment to ask for your help."

"So you still haven't found your magical gold star badge?" Kirsty asked.

Lydia shook her head.

"I'm sure it must be around here somewhere," she said. "Will you please help me find it? Children all over the world have stopped enjoying reading, and it's all because of those terrible goblins."

"Of course we'll help," said Rachel. "Lydia, the goblins are here in the library right now, and no one is watching us. Should we go ask them to give your badge back?"

Lydia nodded.

"I'm a little afraid of Jack Frost, but I'm not scared of goblins," she said. "Let's go talk to them right now."

She hid in Rachel's pocket and then the girls walked back to the tall bookshelf where the goblins were reading.

But before they got there, Kirsty grabbed Rachel's arm.

"Look!" she whispered. "Between those books!"

In a gap between some books on a shelf, the girls could see an ice blue robe and a mortarboard hat. Holding their breath, they tiptoed up to the shelf and peeked through the gap. Then they stared at each other in shock. They couldn't believe their eyes.

Jack Frost was in their school!

A Rhyming Spell and a Reading

Jack Frost was creeping along beside the shelves toward the goblins. They hadn't noticed him because they were so interested in their books. They were still reading aloud.

"The grumpy troll and the handsome goblin snowboarded down the snowy mountain," the first goblin was reading at the top of his voice. "Everyone gasped, because they had never seen such amazing skill and speed.

They were better than Olympic athletes and faster than fairies."

"The goblin found a really great hiding place for the apples," bellowed the second goblin. "But Milly, Tilly, and Jilly cheated and spied on him, and they took the apples back to the orchard. So the goblin locked them in an ice castle for a hundred years, and that served them right."

"BOO!" shouted Jack Frost, leaping out in front of them.

The goblins jumped up in fright, dropping the books on the floor. Jack Frost walked slowly toward them, and they backed away until they hit a bookshelf.

"I'm here for my magical badge," he said. "You little pea brains are going to give it to me—right now!"

He pulled a blue book out from under his robe. Rachel and Kirsty could see the title clearly, because it was written in shining silver letters: *Fantastic Jack Frost: The Story of My Life.*

"This is the best book in the world," he said. "I want every single goblin in my school to hear the story—but none of them are paying attention, and it's all your fault!"

He was shaking with rage, and the
goblins' knees started to knock together.
"W-w-what can we d-d-do, Your

Iciness?" asked the
first goblin.
The second
goblin opened
his mouth
to speak but
couldn't get
any words
out, so he gave
a little curtsy
instead.
"Give me the badge,
fool!" Jack Frost roared.
Trembling, the first goblin put his hand
into his pocket and pulled out a shining
golden badge.

"That's it!" said Lydia. "My badge!"

But before the girls could do anything, Jack Frost had snatched the badge and disappeared in a crack of blue lightning!

"Quick, use your magic!" Rachel begged Lydia. "We have to catch up with Jack Frost!"

Lydia fluttered out of Rachel's pocket and hovered in front of them, holding up her wand and speaking the words of a spell.

"*Follow Jack Frost without any delay*

28

To find the gold badge he has stolen
away.
Whether in sunshine or whether in
snow,
Take us wherever he chooses to go."

With a whooshing sound, a ribbon of
sparkling fairy dust wound
around the girls,
wrapping them
in magic.
They closed
their eyes,
and their
shoulder
blades
tingled as
gossamer
wings appeared.

They heard the tinkle of far-off silver bells and then felt a blast of ice-cold air. When they opened their eyes, they were standing inside a very different kind of library.

Icicles were hanging from the shelves, and there were patches of ice on the threadbare carpet. But the strangest thing was that every book in the library was exactly the same. Row after row, the girls gazed at thousands of copies of a large, blue book with the title written in silver letters. *Fantastic Jack Frost: The Story of My Life*. They were inside the library of Jack Frost's Ice Castle!

The girls and Lydia were standing between two rows of bookshelves. Before they could say a word, they saw Jack Frost striding across the front of the library. A crowd of goblin students was sitting on the carpet in front of him.

"Hide!" said Kirsty with a gasp.

They fluttered over to hide behind a bookshelf at the back of the library, close to the door.

"I thought Jack Frost said that the goblins weren't paying attention," Rachel whispered. "They all look very well-behaved to me."

"There's a good reason for that," said Lydia, looking serious. "Look at what he's wearing on his robe."

The girls peered through the shelves and saw Lydia's magical badge glittering on Jack Frost's robe.

"That's why the goblins are being so good," said Kirsty.

They watched as Jack opened a copy of his book and started to read.

"Chapter one," he began. "The fairies have always caused trouble for me, and their silly sense of right and wrong is always getting in my way. One day, I decided that enough was enough. My brilliant brain instantly thought of a fantastic plan to stop them, once and for all!"

Jack Frost was a very boring reader. He didn't change the tone of his voice at all—he just droned on and on. The girls were soon yawning, but the goblins kept listening as if the story was the most wonderful thing that they had ever heard.

"We have to do something to stop him before we all fall asleep," said Lydia. "We need to get the badge back— but *how*?"

punished!

Rachel looked around and saw a bell hanging on a hook by the library door. She tapped Kirsty on the shoulder and pointed at the bell.

"Jack Frost must ring that bell as the signal for break time," she said. "We'd have a much better chance of getting the badge back from him if the goblins were playing outside. But first, Kirsty and I need to look like goblins."

Lydia held up her wand.

"*Let my spell hide both these faces,*
Cast away all human graces.
Disguise my friends as goblins green,
And let no fairy wings be seen."

The girls felt a creeping, tickling feeling as their clothes were replaced with green goblin uniforms. Their noses and ears grew long and pointy, and their hair shrank away until they were bald.

"Rachel, you look terrible!" said Kirsty with a giggle.

"You, too!" said Rachel, giving her a hug. "I'm glad it's only for a little while."

They made their way over to the library door, hoping that Jack Frost wouldn't see them. Luckily he was still busy reading all about himself. They could hear his voice booming.

"That was when I generously decided to give some goblins the chance to be my servants," he declared. "I visited the goblin village and chose the least foolish and the least ugly of them all. They all kissed my hands in thanks."

"This is definitely not a good story," said Rachel.

She reached up and rang the bell as

loudly as she could. At the front of the library, Jack Frost jumped in surprise and stopped reading. The goblins scrambled to their feet, and there was a stampede for the door.

"Let me out!" Kirsty heard one of them mutter.

"Get me away from this horrible story," whispered another.

"I couldn't stop listening," said a third. "Something was forcing me to be good. It was awful."

They pushed and shoved one another aside, trying to reach the door first. Rachel and Kirsty had to run to get out of their way, but in the confusion they ran in the wrong direction—straight into the arms of Jack Frost!

He pinched one of Kirsty's goblin ears between his thumb and forefinger. He did the same to Rachel, frowning at them.

"I saw what you two did!" he snapped.
"You rang the recess bell too early!
You interrupted the amazing story of
my life! You're going to be punished for
that!"

"We're very sorry," said Kirsty, trying
to whimper like a real goblin. "Please
don't punish us!"

But Jack Frost was furious, and he
wouldn't let go of their ears.

"You will miss out on recess," he said.
"You will have to sit in my office and
work. Come on!"

Rachel and Kirsty exchanged a hopeful
glance. Maybe this was their chance to
get Lydia's badge back!

Pulling Rachel and Kirsty along by the
ears, Jack Frost marched them out of the
library and along a dim, damp hallway

to his office. There was a brass sign on
the door.

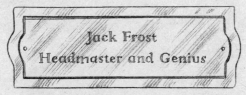

Jack Frost
Headmaster and Genius

By twisting her head around, Rachel
could see that Lydia was hovering behind
them in the shadows. Jack Frost kicked
the door open and shoved the girls inside.
Then he marched around to the chair
behind his desk and sat down. Lydia

just had time to slip
inside the room
before the door
banged shut.
Kirsty saw her
hide behind a
large potted plant.
Above her was a
very droopy cactus.

"You two are going to learn that when
I'm talking, you should be listening," said
Jack Frost, drumming his long fingers on
his desk. "You should have been paying
attention in class. So I want you to write
a whole page each about why *Fantastic
Jack Frost: The Story of My Life* is the
best book ever."

"Oh, thank you, sir!" exclaimed
Kirsty, much to Rachel's surprise.

"That's a wonderful assignment. I could talk for days about your book. It is so exciting! You must be very smart to have written something like that."

A smile flickered around Jack Frost's grumpy mouth, and Rachel suddenly understood Kirsty's idea. If they could distract Jack Frost, Lydia might be able to unpin the badge from his robe.

Hop, Skip, and Jump

"You must have had a really interesting life," said Rachel. "I can't wait to finish reading your amazing book."

"I'm just naturally gifted," said Jack Frost, stroking his spiky beard.

"Will you sign some copies of your book for us?" asked Kirsty, clasping her hands together.

"Well, if you insist," said Jack Frost.

He sounded almost kind. There was
a big pile of his books on the table, and
he opened one and began to sign his
name with a leaking fountain pen. Lydia
swooped down, ducked under his arm,
and started to unfasten the pin. But just as
he finished signing the second book, the
fountain pen squirted a blob of ink onto
Jack Frost's robe. He glanced down—and
saw Lydia trying to take the badge!

"THERE'S A FAIRY IN MY OFFICE?!" bellowed Jack Frost. "How dare you come in here! I'll put you in detention! I'll give you a year's worth of homework! I'll make you take exams every day! COME HERE!"

He tried to trap Lydia between his hands, but she zoomed away from him and out through the open window. Jack Frost hurled himself after her, his long

robe flapping behind him as he ran.

"They're heading for the playground," cried Rachel. "Come on—we have to stop him from catching Lydia!"

She and Kirsty clambered out the window, too, and followed Jack Frost toward the icy playground. He was still yelling at Lydia, but he was so out of shape that he was panting, too. Rachel and Kirsty reached the playground and only just avoided skidding into some goblins playing hopscotch.

"Watch it!" the goblins yelled rudely.

The girls really wanted to say sorry, but they knew that a real goblin would never be that polite! They stuck out their tongues, and so did the other goblins.

"YOWCH!" squealed a tall, lanky goblin.

A plump, warty goblin had landed
on his foot. But as he hopped around,
clutching his toes, he tripped over
a goblin with a jump rope. They
both fell flat on their faces, tangled in
the rope.

"What are you doing?" they screeched
at each other.

Rachel grabbed Kirsty's arm.

"Those clumsy goblins have given me an idea," she said. "Maybe our big goblin feet can trip up Jack Frost."

"Let's try it!" Kirsty said eagerly.

They raced after Jack Frost, who was sprinting around the playground, snatching at the fairy fluttering in front of him. Lydia zigzagged left and right. It was hard to keep up with them, but at last the girls were close enough to touch Jack Frost's trailing robe.

"Ready . . . set . . . JUMP!" shouted Rachel.

They sprang through the air and landed on the hem of the long, blue robe with their big feet. The robe was yanked off Jack Frost, and he staggered sideways,

lost his footing,
and tumbled
into a snowy
sandbox.

Lydia
did a
loop in
mid-air
and
swooped
down to the
robe. She unpinned the
gold star badge before Jack Frost could
clamber to his feet, and then zoomed out
of his reach.

"Give it back!" screamed Jack Frost,
stamping his feet and waving his fists in
the air. "You slimy little fairy! Give me
my badge!"

"It's *my* badge," said Lydia in her gentle voice. "And now that I have it back, thanks to my friends, children all over the world will be able to enjoy reading again."

As she spoke, Rachel and Kirsty's disguises melted away, and they fluttered upward to join Lydia. Jack Frost turned a very strange purple color as he realized he had been tricked. He snatched up his robe, stomped over to the outside bell, and rang it angrily.

"Everyone inside—NOW!" he yelled.
"If I can't have any fun, then neither can
you!"

The goblins grumbled and hung back.
None of them wanted to listen to Jack
Frost reading more from his book. But
their teacher was looking especially
fierce, so one by one they all shuffled
back into the school. Lydia, Kirsty, and
Rachel hovered in the air and watched
them.

"Are we
going to
take the
badge back
to the fairy
school now?"
Kirsty asked, after the
last goblin had gone inside.

"Well . . ." said Lydia. "Maybe it's silly, but I actually feel a little sorry for Jack Frost. After all, he went to all the trouble of writing a book, and now no one wants to read it."

The girls understood how the kind little fairy was feeling.

"Maybe there's something we can do to help," said Rachel. "Should we go back to the library and find out?"

The others nodded, and together they flew back into the goblin school. A terrible noise came from the library. Goblins were squawking, shrieking, and thundering around like a herd of elephants. Jack Frost was sitting at a desk with his head in his hands. Lydia looked around and folded her arms.

"The trouble with these students is that they are bored," she said. "What's the use of a library where every book is the same? I have an idea!" Lydia grinned at Kirsty and Rachel, her eyes twinkling.

The Goblin School Library

Lydia flew up to the center of the ceiling and waved her wand in a wide circle. As a shower of fairy dust rained down onto the library shelves, she recited a spell.

"Transform this room into a place
Of wonderful books and reading space.
Books you read 'til the lights go out.
Books you tell your friends about.

Princesses young and witches old,
Adventures wild and heroes bold.
Books that make you laugh out loud,
Real life tales to make you proud.
Stories that can break your heart.
Stories that are works of art.
Poems, plays, and novels, too.
Fill these dreary shelves anew!"

As she spoke, the endless copies of
Fantastic Jack Frost: The Story of My
Life began to change. One by one, a
colorful selection of books appeared, in
all shapes and sizes. As the goblins started
to notice and talk about it, Jack Frost
looked up. He groaned when he saw all
the copies of his book disappearing.

Rachel and Kirsty flew over to
land on the desk in front of Jack Frost.

He scowled at them.

"What do you want?" he demanded.

"We'd like to have the copies of your book that you signed for us earlier," said Rachel, trying to sound brave.

Jack Frost's mouth fell open. He stared at them for a moment. Then he stood up and hurried to get the books. While he was gone, the goblins grew quieter and quieter. One by one, they were discovering exciting books and settling down to read them. By

the time Jack Frost returned, the goblins were completely quiet.

"There," said Jack Frost, shoving the copies of his book at Rachel and Kirsty.

But he didn't sound quite as angry as usual!

Just then, a very small goblin tapped him on the shoulder.

"I thought you might like this book, sir," said the goblin in a shaky voice.

He held out a copy of *The Snow Queen*. Jack Frost grabbed it and read the back cover.

"Aha!" he exclaimed. "She sounds like my kind of royal!"

He sat down and started reading. With a smile, Lydia landed on the desk beside Rachel and Kirsty.

"You've been wonderful," she said. "Thank you from the bottom of my heart. But now it's time for us all to go home."

The girls kissed her good-bye. Then, in a flurry of magical sparkles, they were lifted into the air. Brushing

fairy dust from their eyes, they blinked
. . . and found themselves sitting in their
classroom at Tippington School.

Everyone was busy writing about
the books they had chosen. Kirsty
and Rachel looked down and smiled.
There was a copy of *Fantastic Jack
Frost: The Story of My Life* in front of
each of them.

"I think it's time to write a book
report!" Rachel whispered.

In a short while, Mr. Beaker cleared his throat.

"All right, everyone," he said. "I'd like to hear what you thought about your books. Let's start with Rachel Walker."

Rachel and Kirsty stood up together.

"We chose the same book," Rachel explained. "It's all about someone named Fantastic Jack Frost. I liked this book because the main character tries to be scary, but sometimes he's very funny without even knowing it."

"I like the way all the characters come to life in the book," Kirsty added. "You could almost believe that Fairyland and the king and queen really do exist."

Rachel shared a secret smile with her best friend.

"Well, it sounds like a really interesting book," said Mr. Beaker. "I've never heard of it before, but you've made me want to read it. I think that the school superintendent will be very impressed with your reports when she visits."

Kirsty and Rachel sat down again as Adam started to read his book report.

"In all the excitement I forgot about the superintendent coming," Rachel whispered. "I hope we can find the last magical gold star badge before she arrives, or the whole visit will go wrong."

Kirsty nodded and gave a little smile. "Don't you know?" she said. "All stories about fairies end happily ever after!"

THE SCHOOL DAY FAIRIES

Rachel and Kirsty found Marissa, Alison,
and Lydia's missing magic badges.
Now it's time for them to help...

Kathryn
the Gym Fairy!

Join their next adventure in this
special sneak peek....

The School Inspector

"I can't believe that tomorrow is our last day at school together," said Kirsty Tate. "It's been a wonderful week—I wish it didn't have to end."

Rachel Walker squeezed her hand as they sat next to each other in the auditorium. The best friends had loved every moment of the past week. Kirsty's school had been flooded, so she had joined Rachel in Tippington.

"It's good that your school will be open again next week, but I am going to miss you so much!" said Rachel.

They were sitting with the rest of Mr. Beaker's class for afternoon assembly. Miss Patel, the principal, clapped her hands together and everyone fell silent.

"Good afternoon, everyone," she said. "I hope that you have all had a good morning and are looking forward to class this afternoon."

"Yes, Miss Patel!" all the students said together.

"Some of you have already met our school superintendent, Mrs. Best," Miss Patel went on. "She is observing the school today and tomorrow."

A lady with a clipboard joined Miss Patel at the front of the auditorium, and everyone clapped politely.

"I hope that you will all continue to show Mrs. Best what a wonderful school this is," said Miss Patel.

Just then, Rachel and Kirsty heard the sound of chattering nearby. They peered along their row and saw two boys in green uniforms, snickering and muttering to each other. The girls exchanged a knowing glance. They knew that the boys were goblins in disguise.

RAINBOW magic ™

Which Magical Fairies Have You Met?

- ❏ The Rainbow Fairies
- ❏ The Weather Fairies
- ❏ The Jewel Fairies
- ❏ The Pet Fairies
- ❏ The Dance Fairies
- ❏ The Music Fairies
- ❏ The Sports Fairies
- ❏ The Party Fairies
- ❏ The Ocean Fairies
- ❏ The Night Fairies
- ❏ The Magical Animal Fairies
- ❏ The Princess Fairies
- ❏ The Superstar Fairies
- ❏ The Fashion Fairies
- ❏ The Sugar & Spice Fairies
- ❏ The Earth Fairies
- ❏ The Magical Crafts Fairies
- ❏ The Baby Animal Rescue Fairies
- ❏ The Fairy Tale Fairies
- ❏ The School Day Fairies

▲ SCHOLASTIC

Find all of your favorite fairy friends at
scholastic.com/rainbowmagic

HIT entertainment

RMFAIRY

RAINBOW magic™

Magical fun for everyone!
Learn fairy secrets, send friendship notes, and more!

■ SCHOLASTIC

HIT entertainment

www.scholastic.com/rainbowmagic

RMACTIV4

RAINBOW magic™

Which Magical Fairies Have You Met?

- ☐ Joy the Summer Vacation Fairy
- ☐ Holly the Christmas Fairy
- ☐ Kylie the Carnival Fairy
- ☐ Stella the Star Fairy
- ☐ Shannon the Ocean Fairy
- ☐ Trixie the Halloween Fairy
- ☐ Gabriella the Snow Kingdom Fairy
- ☐ Juliet the Valentine Fairy
- ☐ Mia the Bridesmaid Fairy
- ☐ Flora the Dress-Up Fairy
- ☐ Paige the Christmas Play Fairy
- ☐ Emma the Easter Fairy
- ☐ Cara the Camp Fairy
- ☐ Destiny the Rock Star Fairy
- ☐ Belle the Birthday Fairy
- ☐ Olympia the Games Fairy

- ☐ Selena the Sleepover Fairy
- ☐ Cheryl the Christmas Tree Fairy
- ☐ Florence the Friendship Fairy
- ☐ Lindsay the Luck Fairy
- ☐ Brianna the Tooth Fairy
- ☐ Autumn the Falling Leaves Fairy
- ☐ Keira the Movie Star Fairy
- ☐ Addison the April Fool's Day Fairy
- ☐ Bailey the Babysitter Fairy
- ☐ Natalie the Christmas Stocking Fairy
- ☐ Lila and Myla the Twins Fairies
- ☐ Chelsea the Congratulations Fairy
- ☐ Carly the School Fairy
- ☐ Angelica the Angel Fairy
- ☐ Blossom the Flower Girl Fairy
- ☐ Skyler the Fireworks Fairy

3 stories in each one!

■ SCHOLASTIC

Find all of your favorite fairy friends at
scholastic.com/rainbowmagic

HIT entertainment

RMSPECIAL1